D0908404

DR. PREN
AND THE ATTACK
OF THE GERMS

....

MÁXIMO CÉSAR CASTELLANOS

EDITORIAL RAMY

Georgetown, Delaware

Editorial Ramy
Georgetown, Delaware

Publisher's Note: This is a work of fiction. Names, characters, places, and incidents are a product of the author's imagination. Public names and places are sometimes used for atmospheric purposes. Any resemblance to actual people, living or dead, or to businesses, companies, events, institutions, or places is completely coincidental.

Book Layout © BookDesignTemplates.com
Cover designed by Rafido

DR. PREN AND THE ATTACK OF THE GERMS
Máximo César Castellanos
First Edition, 2021
ISBN 978-0-578-94980-2
Printed in the United States of America

Contents

This book is dedicated to Mr. Mark J. Record

for all his encouragement and support.

"He who is hard to please,

may get nothing in the end."

CHAPTER ONE

....

ONE DAY AT WORK

In the beginning, everything was red. The red turned into wine. The wine was being poured into a glass.

George was asleep on his couch when suddenly the sun's rays covered his face. George woke up right away. I'll be late for work, he thought. George ran out of his house so fast he didn't notice the mailman's presence and bumped into him. All the mail went flying through the air. George apologized to the mailman and left. On his way to work, George grabbed a piece of bread and tossed a coin at the baker as he went by the bakery. Minutes later, George arrived at the bar.

"Just look who it is, the man who lost the bet," said an old lady. Then, she grabbed the glass and drank the red wine.

"Remember that you have to pay the bet or you will lose your life. The good thing is that Don Ponanso gave you until Saturday to find out all about Dr. Pren's life," said his boss.

"There is still hope. Dr. Pren assured me that he would tell me all about his life by Saturday," said George.

"I think I'll call the funeral home," said the old lady laughing.

"You're wrong. Dr. Pren is a great man. He saved the world from total destruction," said George.

"Are you sure? I haven't heard anything about him," said his boss.

"Do you want a drink? I mean, while you're still alive," said his boss laughing.

"Shut up," said George.

"Why? Look what trouble you've gotten yourself into for being so curious," said his boss, "Haven't you heard the saying, 'Curiosity killed the cat'?"

The teasing continued for the rest of the day.

"I think I should put up a sign that says 'Help Wanted'," said his boss.

"Enough!" yelled George, "If you don't leave me alone, I'll quit."

"Do you want to bet?" asked his boss laughing.

George came out of the bar and slammed the door shut.

"Come back. We were having fun," yelled his boss.

George looked at his watch. It was time to visit Dr. Pren. George crossed the street and knocked on the door of the little cabin. The door opened.

"You're back," said Dr. Pren.

"Well, you haven't told me everything about your life," said George.

"Do you want to hear more about my life?" asked Dr. Pren.

"Why do you think I'm here?" asked George.

"Well, where were we . . . I remember now," said Dr. Pren, *"I was nine years old and I'd gone to live with another family . . ."*

CHAPTER TWO

....

THE PETS

*L*ike I told you yesterday, there were three boys in the family, Carl, Elijah, and Jay. They weren't bad people. We lived in a small apartment in the city. The three boys were rarely home, and they never told me where they went. I continued working every day to create a living pet. But as you can imagine, without much success. Every now and then I thought of the Thups, my adoptive parents. "When will they come for me?" I asked myself. That's how my life was until I turned 17 years old.

When Elijah turned 20 years old, his father gave him a truck. The boys used the truck a lot the first month, but they *suddenly stopped using it and hid it behind the apartment building where we lived. Since nobody used the truck, I decided to hide a small crossbow and a container in the truck. The container had the formula I had created to destroy Xephermous when I was six years old. The formula could destroy anything.*

One day, as I was walking behind an animal market close to where we lived, I saw some people throwing away animal parts in a dumpster. I decided to pick up a heart they had thrown away and use it to create my pet. I continued to return to the animal market for more animal parts. Creating a pet had become a very disgusting job.

Finally, one day I was able to create a small and cute pet. The pet was a purple furball with adorable eyes and little gray arms and legs. It was a dream come true. I was about to hug it when suddenly, it exploded.

At that moment, I heard the sirens of police cars. Immediately, the three boys entered the room. They were all wearing masks.

"What's going on?" I asked.

"We never told you, but we're graffiti artists," said Jay.

"What is that?" I asked.

"We're basically artists. We express our emotions through paintings on any wall of the city, but our art is not appreciated by all people," said Carl.

"Sounds interesting. Can you teach me?" I asked.

"Of course, but you will to have to wait until tomorrow," said Carl.

"All right," I said.

The next day, before I left to go with the boys, I went to the truck, poured some of the formula into the small crossbow, and placed it in one of my pants pockets. I wanted to be prepared in case I ran into a problem.

Once I was ready, I went with the boys to learn how to do graffiti and express my emotions. We found a perfect place. It was a massive wall behind a building. We all started painting on the wall with spray paint. I felt like a graffiti artist with cans of spray paint in my hands. But I didn't understand why we had to wear masks all the time. Then, one day I was painting a wall when I heard a voice.

"Leave the can of spray paint on the ground and turn around slowly," said the voice.

I put the can of spray paint on the ground, and when I turned around, I saw it was a policeman. I noticed that the boys were gone. The policeman put me in his police car.

"Your name," said the policeman.

"Dr. Pren," I said.

"Your full name," said the policeman.

"Dr. Pren," I said again.

"I'm not playing," said the policeman.

"Neither am I," I said.

The policeman grabbed my hand, took my fingerprints with a device, and tried to find information about me in his database.

"Unbelievable! It looks like your fingerprints have never been registered in the system," said the policeman.

"Good for me!" I said.

"Do you have any identification?" asked the policeman.

"What is that?" I asked.

"Something that says who you are," said the policeman.

"How am I supposed to know," I said.

"Boy, are you saying that there's no document that indicates who you are?" asked the policeman.

"I don't know," I said.

"You know, this means you can go wherever you want, you can do whatever you want, and nobody would know," said the policeman. "Unfortunately for you, I have your fingerprints now. When I press this button, your information will be uploaded to our database. From now on, if you do something wrong, we'll know you did it."

At that moment, I remembered that I was carrying my most precious weapon with me. *I put my hand in my pants pocket and pulled out the little crossbow. I pointed it at the policeman's finger and shot the formula before the policeman pressed the button.*

The policeman's hand began to turn into ashes. Right away, I shot the floor of the police car so that I could get away. Immediately, the policeman and the police car completely turned into ashes. Now I was sitting in the middle of a pile of ashes on the street.

"How did that happen?" asked Jay as he stepped out of the shadow of an alley accompanied by his brothers.

"I used a weapon I invented when I was little," I said.

"To be clear, we have always thought you were cool," said Elijah.

"There's nothing to be afraid of," I said.

"Should we go back home?" asked Carl.

"Let's go back," said Elijah.

When we got home, I decided to work on my pet again.

"Hey, you've never told us what you're working on," said Jay.

"I'm trying to create a living pet," I said.

"Wouldn't it be easier to buy one at the pet store?" asked Elijah.

"Maybe, but this pet is going to be special and different than any other," I said.

"Where did you get the stuff to create your pet?" asked Carl.

"I started by picking up a heart that had been discarded behind the animal market and put it in my pet," I said.

"Are you saying that you've taken discarded body parts from that animal market?" asked Jay.

"Sure, where else would I get real animal parts?" I asked.

"Do you know that those animal parts may be infected?" asked Carl.

"I don't care," I said.

I was about to create another pet. I gave its heart an electric shock. Immediately, my pet's heart started beating, and a few seconds later, it started breathing. Then, I noticed one of its fingers was moving. It blinked and then it stared at us. It began to get up slowly and then it sat down. I hugged it and jumped with joy.

"I'll call you Gilbert," I said.

Over the next few days, we taught Gilbert how to walk and do tricks. Sometime later, I thought, since I succeeded in creating one pet, I could certainly create another one.

My second pet would also be fuzzy like Gilbert, but it would be white instead of purple. Its arms and legs would be blue instead of gray so that I could tell it apart from Gilbert.

One day, I was working on my new pet when I saw Gilbert arrive with a giant brain. I didn't know where he got it from, but I decided to use it to create my new pet.

This time I was able to create my second living pet in just a few days. My new pet was the female version of Gilbert. I called her Patty.

I didn't know it then, but Gilbert's heart was infected. The infection began to change Gilbert. After a few days of playing with Gilbert and Patty, I decided to go again with the boys to paint the city walls. Some days I played with my pets, and other days I would go out with the boys to paint the city walls. The boys had finally accepted me and included me in their activities. At last, I had

14

my own pets and felt the unconditional love that only pets can give you.

But everything changed one day. After going to paint for a little while with the boys, I came home. I couldn't find Gilbert or Patty anywhere. Finally, I found them on the roof of the building where we lived.

"Thank GOD you're all right. You shouldn't be here," I said.

"Get away, human," said Gilbert.

"I didn't know you could talk," I said.

"I see you don't know much because you don't know that you have to feed us either," said Gilbert.

"You're right. I completely forgot. Why don't we go down? I'll give you both some corn," I said.

"We don't eat corn," said Gilbert.

"What do you eat?" I asked.

"People's health," said Gilbert.

"I don't understand," I said.

"I'm not the pet you thought you created. I am a germ," said Gilbert. "I absorb

people's health and replace their health with a disease."

"Is Patty a germ too?" I asked.

"She's not, but thanks to the huge brain you put in her, Patty can control the weather," said Gilbert.

"What do you plan to do?" I asked.

"Grow," said Patty smiling.

I took out my crossbow and shot the formula at Patty. Patty invoked a lightning bolt. The lightning bolt struck right in front of her blocking the formula. The lightning bolt turned into ashes. I don't know how she grew so much, but Patty was almost as tall as me. I was about to shoot the formula at her again when Patty jumped off the roof and disappeared.

Gilbert walked towards me. My body shook as I thought Gilbert would absorb my health. I pointed my crossbow at Gilbert. I was about to shoot him when I noticed that my crossbow had run out of formula. I ran away quickly, went down the stairs, and headed for the truck.

When I got to the parking lot, the truck was gone. I ran down the street and saw a tow truck taking it away. I ran after the tow truck because the only formula left in the world was in that truck. I chased the tow truck to the outskirts of town. The tow truck kept going farther and farther away. I think I lost some weight that day because I ran a lot. Finally, the tow truck reached a town far away from the city.

I chased the tow truck to an impound lot. I approached the office window and heard some people planning to steal more cars to then sell them. I went to the truck and tried to remove the chains tying the truck to the tow truck while the people discussed the price of the truck. I couldn't take the chains off the truck. Then, I had an idea.

I filled my crossbow with the formula and shot the chains. The chains turned into ashes. In that moment, I realized someone was behind me.

CHAPTER THREE

....

THE ROBBERY

"*W*hy are you stealing our truck?" asked one of the robbers.

"This is Elijah's truck. You stole it from him," I said.

"You're just a baby. No one will believe you," said the robber.

"I'll call the police," I said.

"I am a police officer. If you call the police, my phone will ring, and I won't help you," said the robber.

I didn't know what to do, so I looked all around. Then, I had an idea. I grabbed a rock from the floor and threw it at the robber. The rock went right by the robber's face.

"You missed," said the robber.

The rock struck a bucket full of water and knocked it down. The water spilled everywhere and wet some wires that were on the floor causing a short circuit that started a fire. The flames set fire to a barrel that was close to the cables. The fire became larger, releasing hot air towards the ceiling.

The hot air pushed up a toy plane that was hanging by a thread from the roof. The toy plane began to spin. The more hot air that was released by the fire, the faster the toy plane spun. The toy plane spun so fast that one of its wings cut the thread that held a hammer hanging from the ceiling. The hammer fell on a box of razor blades. The razor blades flew through the air cutting more threads that held other hammers hanging from the ceiling. Since the hammers were right on top of the robbers, they fell on the heads of the robbers, knocking them unconscious.

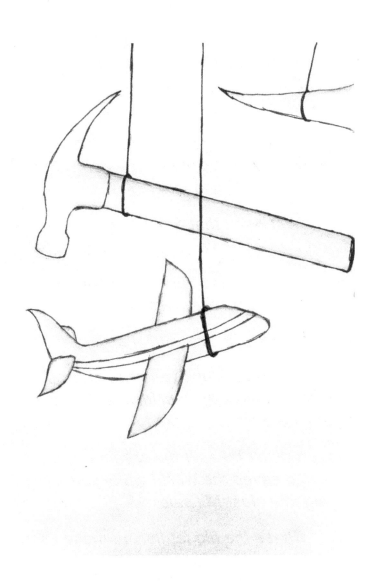

"Thank you for decorating the workshop this way," I said.

Then, I saw other people running towards me. Just before they grabbed me, they all fell to the floor unconscious. Behind the people were two women.

"Do you remember me, Dr. Pren?" asked one of the women. She had yellow hair and was very thin.

"Were you that fan who asked for my autograph a few years ago?" I asked.

"I would never ask for an idiot's autograph," said the woman.

"Then, who are you?" I asked.

"I'm Alice. Don't you remember that I helped you save the world, and then you took all the credit?" asked Alice.

"I didn't take all the credit. I was the one who saved the world while you were crying in a closet," I said.

"That's the big fat lie you made up. I expected something better from you. It doesn't matter anymore," said Alice.

"This is my friend Wanda," said Alice.

I looked at Wanda. She was a little shorter than Alice and had black hair.

"What are you doing here?" I asked.

"What does it look like? Saving your life," said Alice.

"But how did you know that I was going to be here?" I asked.

"That doesn't matter. The important thing is that you tell us what we're up against this time," said Alice.

"We're up against a germ that absorbs people's health and replaces it with a disease," I said, "The germ saw how I created my second pet Patty, so now it is probably creating more germs. If we don't hurry up, they'll spread throughout the world."

"I took a look at the container that keeps the formula that you have in the truck, and it seems to be almost empty. You need to create more formula. Do you remember how to do it?" asked Alice.

"Well, it's just that, actually . . ." I started to say.

"Did you lie again?" asked Alice.

"Maybe I exaggerated a few things. Well, maybe I exaggerated the whole thing," I said.

"It doesn't matter. I created a backup plan just in case you were lying," said Alice.

"Well, actually, I created 236 backup plans," said Alice.

"You have 236 backup plans?" I asked.

"We also have some backup plans for the backup plans," said Wanda.

"Let's focus! I heard a company is creating a formula that instantly turns houses into ashes. Supposedly, they will use it to demolish old houses quickly and without causing any noise. I heard they were going to finish creating it in a week. So, we'll steal the formula in a week," said Alice.

"We don't have that much time," I said.

"We need time to hire people to help us fight the germs and to locate where the company is creating the formula, so just calm down," said Alice.

"I just don't know what to do," I said.

"I know what to do. Let's wait a week and then steal the formula," said Wanda.

Then, we went to Alice's house. While Wanda and Alice worked, I decided to lie down on the couch to watch TV.

After a week, Wanda had already hired 20 people, and Alice had finally located the building where they were creating the new formula.

That night, I built some crossbows and gave each person one with only a few drops of the formula that was left. One of the people that Wanda had hired was very good with computers. He hacked the building's security system, and we managed to get in.

It looked as if a beast had destroyed the whole place. There were pieces of glass on the floor and holes in the walls.

Suddenly, we heard a scream. I followed the scream to the women's restroom. There was a little girl inside.

"What happened here?" I asked.

"A week ago, my dad received the news that there were some creatures attacking people. He created a formula to stop them. He lied to everyone. He told them that it was a formula to destroy old houses," said the little girl. "My dad brought me here today to show me the formula, but the creatures came out of nowhere and attacked us. I don't know where my dad is."

"Where's the formula?" I asked.

"The formula is on the top floor. To get in, you need to deactivate the alarm from the control room," said the little girl.

I picked up the little girl and gave her to Wanda.

"Take the little girl to the police and ask them to take her to her mom," I told Wanda.

After Wanda left with the little girl, I told everyone what the little girl had told me.

We found the control room and saw a man lying on the floor. Luckily, he was still breathing. He had some strange marks on his face, and he looked very sick. We *deactivated the alarm and called the hospital to send an ambulance.*

We went to the top floor and found the formula in a container. I put some of the formula in each of our crossbows. It got mixed with the formula that was already in the crossbows. I shot a door and the door turned into ashes. It works! Now we were ready. When we left the building, we were surrounded by cops.

The cops confiscated all our weapons. As I got in the police car, I saw a germ peeking out of the door of the building. The germ looked right into my eyes. Suddenly, a dozen germs appeared right behind him. All of the germs were of different sizes and some of them had fur that was darker than the others. Apparently, the more health they absorbed from people, the bigger, the stronger, the more aggressive, and the more dangerous they became.

It looked like the entire time we were inside the building, the germs were in there with us. But for some reason, they didn't attack us. It was as if they wanted the police to detain us. Perhaps the germs knew that we were the only people with weapons capable of destroying them.

CHAPTER FOUR

....

THE JUDGEMENT

T he next day, they took us to a huge room. Apparently, the robbery was more serious than I thought. There were a lot of television reporters. There were also people representing different companies.

A man in some ridiculous clothes came into the room and sat down behind a desk that had a little hammer.

"Mr. Pen, you stole the . . ." started to say the man in ridiculous clothes.

"My name is Dr. Pren," I said.

"That doesn't matter. Now, can you explain to me why you stole the formula?" asked the man in ridiculous clothes.

"Not until you tell me why my name doesn't matter," I replied.

"Here sir, you speak to me with respect," said the man in ridiculous clothes.

"Why don't we all go home and forget everything that happened?" I asked.

"That is why we are here. I'll decide whether you're going home or you're going to jail," said the man in ridiculous clothes.

"Actually, my house is just a cold little room with a bed, and jail is the same, so I don't care," I said.

"But there's a television in your house, isn't there?" asked the man in ridiculous clothes.

"Yes," I answered.

"There is also delicious food in your house, isn't there?" asked the man in ridiculous clothes.

"Yes," I answered.

"Then, apparently your house is better than jail," said the man in ridiculous clothes.

"Then, if you know my house is better, why don't you let me go home?" I asked.

"So, you can learn that in this country there are laws and you have to respect them," said the man in ridiculous clothes.

"Just like you respect my name, I suppose," I said.

"Why are you so disrespectful?" asked the man in ridiculous clothes.

"The Bible says 'treat others as you want to be treated,' so if you treat others disrespectfully, others will treat you disrespectfully," I said.

Everyone in the room started talking about what was going on.

"Order!" shouted the man in ridiculous clothes slamming his little hammer on the desk.

"Are we supposed to shut up when you hit that little hammer? Because the last time I hit a hammer, no one shut up," I said.

"Order!" shouted the man in ridiculous clothes.

"Why are you shouting 'order'? It's not like we are in court," I asked.

"In court is exactly where you are," said the man in ridiculous clothes.

"Why didn't anyone tell me I was in court?" I asked.

"I told you three times when we got here," whispered Alice.

"Does that mean I'm going to jail after this?" I asked.

"You will if you don't tell me what happened," replied the man in ridiculous clothes.

Then, I explained everything exactly the way it happened. After that, I waited a few seconds until finally he spoke to me again.

"I know you're lying to me," said the man in ridiculous clothes.

"Of course not," I answered.

"If you don't tell me the truth, I'll send you to jail," said the man in ridiculous clothes.

That threat reminded me of an incident that happened eight years ago. I clearly remembered the teacher saying something similar to my best friend, Adam, on that occasion.

"I know you're lying," the teacher had told Adam.

"No. There must be a mistake," Adam had replied.

"If you don't tell me the truth, I'll send you to the principal's office," the teacher had told Adam.

This caused Adam to become so angry that his anger made him develop supernatural powers.

In my case, I knew I wasn't going to develop any kind of power, so I had to change my strategy if I wanted to go home. I looked around the courtroom and pointed at the first representative of a company I saw.

"He forced me to steal the formula to make more profit. I was a victim, and he's the one to blame," I lied to the man in ridiculous clothes, "I swear."

The man in ridiculous clothes believed the lie, and the police arrested the company representative. As I left the courtroom, Alice came up to me.

"It's not good to lie. The Bible says that too," said Alice.

"What was I supposed to say? He was going to put me in jail," I said.

"But you know what the truth is, and no one wins anything by telling lies," said Alice.

"I won my freedom," I said.

"You don't understand," said Alice and she left.

The police gave us back our weapons. It was time to start exterminating those germs.

We transformed Alice's house into a base and built motorcycles with super turbines.

The first place we went was to the building where we had stolen the new formula. We quickly eliminated half of the germs and captured the other half to study them. I set up an underground security system, and that's where we locked up the germs.

"Look how many we've already captured," I said.

"But don't forget there are lots more in the city," said Alice.

CHAPTER FIVE

....

THE ATTACK OF THE GERMS

*I*t took longer than we thought to locate all the germs. Once we had located them, we built five other bases at different strategic points surrounding all the places where the germs were located.

I designed a transportation system that connected all of the bases underground. We all had credentials with special chips that allowed access to secret passageways located inside portable bathrooms. People were transported underground on small rockets to the closest base. I designed weapons that shot faster and farther. I also designed suits to protect us from the germs.

Over the next few months, we saved many lives and destroyed many germs.

"If we keep this up, we'll eliminate all the germs within the next two months," I said.

"I don't think that will be possible," said Alice.

"Why not?" I asked.

"Look out the window," said Alice.

When I looked out the window, hundreds of germs started to appear.

"Where did they come from?" I asked.

"I don't know. They appeared out of nowhere. Now the number of germs has doubled," said Alice.

"Gilbert is not capable of creating hundreds of germs in such a short amount of time," I said.

I went out and started destroying the germs, but there were so many. I couldn't eliminate all of them. I ran back to the base and closed the door. Unfortunately, that day was New Year's Day, so half of the workers had the day off.

I went to my office and pressed a button on my desk. An alarm started sounding. Steve and Windor, two of the workers, came down from the second floor. I asked them to destroy as many germs as they could.

Then, I remembered we had captured germs to examine. I went out into the backyard and opened a metal door that was on the ground. I went downstairs and entered a huge room where there was a gigantic computer. I typed the password on the computer, and a wall opened. There was a pool on the other side of the wall. I went into the pool and swam to the other end where there was a wooden door. I came out of the pool, opened the wooden door, and entered a hallway.

As I ran down the hallway, arrows flew out of the walls, but I was able to dodge them. I got to a metal door and opened it. On the other side of the metal door, there was a computer and an elevator with the doors closed. I typed the password on the computer, and the elevator doors opened.

I entered the elevator and it took me deeper. Soon after, the elevator stopped and the doors opened. I had finally reached the room where we were keeping the germs. I just wanted to see you all and make sure none of you had escaped, I thought.

Suddenly, the roof collapsed, and a bunch of germs started coming in. I went into the elevator. I went back through the hallway, swam back through the pool, went up the stairs as fast as I could, went back to my office, and locked myself in it.

I sat in my chair and took a deep breath. I tried to calm down, so I could think about what to do. Suddenly, germ hands started breaking through the floor. I screamed and jumped out of my chair. Some of the germ hands grabbed my chair and pulled it down, making a hole in the floor.

I ran towards the entrance. Germ hands came out of the floor with every step I took. Then, a germ broke through the floor and stood in front of me. It was about to grab me when Steve came out of nowhere and shot it, but he missed. The germ changed his attention towards Steve.

Steve shot again, but the germ ripped up a piece of the floor and used it as a shield. When the formula hit the piece of floor, it turned into ashes. The germ jumped towards Steve, grabbed him, and threw him towards a wall. The germ had thrown him so hard that Steve flew out of the base and went through eight houses. Steve was unconscious in the middle of the living room of the eighth house.

Meanwhile, I was still inside my office with the germ. I thought about shooting the germ when I realized my weapon was on the other side of the room. I ran towards my weapon when suddenly the germ grabbed me and threw me on the floor.

The germ got on top of me and opened its huge mouth. I tried to grab my weapon, but the germ was holding my arms. I saw 14 rows of teeth in the germ's mouth. Tentacles started coming out of its mouth. The tentacles began to wrap around my head as the germ got its mouth closer and closer to my head.

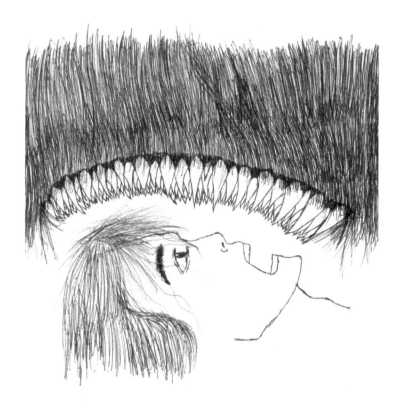

There were many holes in the floor of my office made by the germs that had escaped. The floor could no longer support our weight and collapsed.

The germ let go of me. Unfortunately, I fell in the middle of hundreds of germs. I thought that would be my end. Then, I had an idea. I pointed to the right and yelled, "A butterfly!"

All of the germs turned to look for the butterfly which allowed me to escape.

I left the base, but I didn't know what to do. I found Alice, Windor, and Steve, already recovered, hiding behind a tree.

"I don't have a weapon," I said.

"The only one with a weapon is Windor, mine got lost, and Steve's broke," said Alice.

"I wonder where all those germs came from," said Steve.

We saw how the germs destroyed the base.

"You do have insurance, don't you?" I asked.

"Are you asking me that now?" asked Alice.

Windor started shooting at some germs. A germ came out from behind us and grabbed Windor. I took Windor's weapon immediately. The weapon was covered in sweat, so it took me a little while to operate it.

At last, I was able to shoot the germ that was attacking Windor. Windor stood up. He had the same marks on his face as the other germs' victims, but he didn't seem to be sick.

"Do we take you to the hospital?" I asked.

"I don't know. I don't feel sick, but I am feeling something that I've never felt before," said Windor.

I looked at the marks on his face. They reminded me of something.

"I think I know what those marks on your face mean," I said.

"What do they mean?" asked Windor.

"The marks appear to be symbols written in a language created by humans, but no human can read it," I said.

"I don't understand," said Alice.

We went to the nearest store. When we walked in, we went straight to the cashier and scanned Windor's face with the barcode scanner. A message appeared on the screen of the scanner.

The message said, 'If you destroy the King of the Germs, all the germs will disappear.'

"Gilbert must be the King of the Germs," I said.

"How will we know which germ is Gilbert?" asked Alice.

"The problem is that they all look alike," I said.

"But maybe he's the biggest, the strongest, the most aggressive and the most dangerous one," said Alice.

"There's no time to lose! Let's go in search of the King of the Germs," I said.

CHAPTER SIX

....

IN THE DARKNESS

*T*hat afternoon, we decided to go and stay at Steve's house. Steve lived with his wife and daughter.

During dinner, Steve said, "Something I never understood was how the germs can stand on their legs. Their legs are so thin and have almost no muscle."

"That's because their bodies are not as heavy as they look," I said. "Their legs are placed in specific places that allow them to maintain their balance while standing."

"If you pay attention, when the germs run, they fall continuously. Every time they

fall, their feet push against the ground, lifting them up again," I said.

"What are you going to do about all the new germs?" asked Steve's wife.

"We'll have to start from zero," I said. "It's like a video game, in which we've lost all our lives. Now, we have to start over from the beginning."

At that moment, Steve's daughter went over to her mom and whispered in her ear.

"All right," said her mom and her daughter ran off.

"What did she tell you?" asked Windor.

"She forgot her toy outside the house and asked if she could go out and get it," said Steve's wife.

"It's not safe outside," I said. I stood up right away and went after the girl.

The girl was picking up her toy in the middle of the backyard when she heard a branch break. She couldn't see anything because it was nighttime. The girl walked *towards the noise. Right in front of her was a germ.*

The germ came out of the darkness. The girl screamed. Just before the germ grabbed her, I pulled her away from the germ. I held her in my arms and grabbed a stick that was on the ground. The germ immediately hid behind some bushes in the darkness. I started hearing footsteps around me. I didn't dare turn my back on the germ and try to run to the house.

The germ probably expected me to do that so it could attack us. I took a step back. Then, I heard something behind me. I turned quickly, but I didn't see anything. The darkness covered everything around me. Chills went up my spine. The wind was blowing the leaves of the trees.

If I was scared, I couldn't imagine how the girl felt. I picked up the girl and held her in my arms. She was gripping the toy tightly, trying to hide in my arms, and not see what was happening. Immediately, I ran away from the house. As I ran, I could hear branches breaking and the rustle of the tree leaves and shrubs. Suddenly, everything went silent. Then, we started hearing footsteps approaching us. I kept running until I reached a completely desolate street. I could feel the cold air hitting my face. I stared into the trees thinking something would come out from behind them, but nothing happened. I kept running down the street for what seemed like an eternity.

Finally, I stopped running and I took a look at the girl. She was asleep. The girl was wearing a watch on her wrist. I saw it was almost midnight.

I walked a little bit more. Then, I saw Elijah's truck approaching us. The truck stopped in front of us. Alice's neighbor got out of the truck.

"I didn't want the germs to take your truck. So, I took it," said the neighbor.

"How far are we from your home?" I asked.

"I don't know. I am trying to escape from the germs, but they're everywhere," said the neighbor.

"One of our bases is nearby," I said.

I put the girl in the truck and I climbed up on the roof of the truck where the cannons were. I wanted to be prepared in case a germ attacked us. We didn't see any germs on the way.

There were four workers inside the base when we got there.

"Has anything out of the ordinary happened here today?" I asked one of the workers.

"No, nothing. Now that I think about it, we haven't seen any germs all day," replied a worker.

I told them what had happened to us.

"It seems like the germs intended to destroy the main base. Perhaps they are trying to destroy the bases one at a time," said the worker.

"It's likely," I said. "We'll spend the night here."

"Of course. Clara will take you to your rooms," said the worker.

"I need to make a call," I said.

I called Steve to tell him that his daughter was safe and sound, that we would spend the night at the base, and that we would see them in the morning.

That night after I laid down, I began to have that feeling of loneliness similar to the one I had in a vision when I was a child. I had felt lonely for most of my life. That's why I created a pet.

At that moment, I realized that I was solely responsible for everything that had happened.

I tried to think of a way to destroy all the germs. I didn't know how much Gilbert had changed physically, but I did know that he had become bigger, stronger, more aggressive and more dangerous.

It was evident that Gilbert was responsible for the creation of all the germs. It became obvious that the only way to save the world from the germs was by destroying Gilbert.

Where's Gilbert? Where's Patty? How did Gilbert create so many germs so quickly? So many questions crossed my mind.

The next day, I called Alice.

"Dr. Pren, good thing you called. We found something very strange last night. I think it's Patty," said Alice.

"Where are you?" I asked.

"We're in the laundromat in the town of Milworm," said Alice. "Come quickly. We need you."

I looked at the time on the clock. It was eight in the morning.

"How long does it take to get to the town of Milworm from here?" I asked Clara.

"Well, by car, it takes . . ." started to say Clara.

"Perfect," I interrupted her. "To start, call Steve to tell him that I'll send his daughter back home with one of the workers. Then, give me four weapons and come with me. An old friend is waiting for us at the Milworm laundromat," I said.

Clara and I got in the truck.

"I brought a motorcycle just in case," I said.

"I brought five crossbows and a map," said Clara.

"Milworm is about ..." started to say Clara.

"Three inches from here ..." I interrupted her. *"It won't take long for us to get there then."*

It was almost noon, and we hadn't arrived yet.

"I think the map is wrong," I said, *"It was supposed to be only three inches."*

"You interrupted me when I was calculating the distance," said Clara.

Hours later, we finally got to Milworm. Unfortunately, we arrived during the night.

I got out of the truck and walked to the laundromat. The wind was blowing hard and moving the thick trees that surrounded the laundromat. When I went into the laundromat, the lights were on. The place was spotless, but there was no one there.

"Don't tell me that Clara brought us to the wrong town," I said.

Suddenly, something moved behind me. I turned around, but I didn't see anything. Afterward, I heard someone say my name. I looked from side to side, then Patty appeared right in front of me.

"Now I wish that Clara had gotten the wrong town," I said.

"Why so lonely, Dr. Pren?" asked Patty.

"I'm not alone. My friends are here with me," I said.

"Don't you understand? Sooner or later, everyone will be against you. One day, there will be a whole army fighting against you. I'll ask you again, why so lonely, Dr. Pren?" said Patty.

"I would never do anything bad to my friends," I said.

"What about Mr. Hopper?" asked Patty.

"I made a lot of mistakes when I was a kid," I said.

"And you'll keep making them," said Patty.

"I don't want to hear anymore," I said as I pulled a crossbow out of my pocket.

I shot the formula at Patty, but a lightning bolt struck right in front of her. The formula hit the lightning bolt and turned it into ashes.

Patty snapped her fingers. I looked outside of the laundromat. The most amazing thing I'd ever seen suddenly appeared. A gigantic monster made entirely of wind was right outside, in front of the laundromat.

"Do you like my hurricane?" asked Patty.

"It's made of air, another thing my weapon can't destroy," I said, "but all that air is controlled by something."

"You're smart," said Patty.

"If it's a hurricane, then the source of power that attracts all the air is in the eye of the hurricane," I said.

"As I said, you're very smart," said Patty.

"Something that I know and you don't know," said Patty, *"is that the formula you use to destroy things . . ."*

Patty turned into ashes immediately. Alice, Steve, and Windor were standing behind the ashes.

"Couldn't you have waited a little longer? She was about to tell me something important," I said.

"Windor was the one who shot her," said Steve.

"I didn't know she was about to say something important," said Windor.

"Never mind, now we have to figure out how to destroy the hurricane," I said.

When I turned around to look outside the laundromat, the hurricane was gone.

"Do you think the hurricane disappeared when we destroyed Patty?" asked Steve.

"No, that hurricane is still out there. It just got away because it knew we'd go after it once we destroyed Patty," I said.

"How are we going to find it?" asked Steve.

"I don't think it'll be hard to find a giant monster made out of air just walking around," I said.

But I wasn't sure if we could find it. We got in the truck anyway and went looking for it. As we drove through Milworm, we saw that some trees had been knocked down, and the mall had been destroyed.

"It looks like the hurricane passed through here," I said.

CHAPTER SEVEN

....

THE HURRICANE

"*T*his is not good at all," said Alice.

We continued driving through the streets in search of the hurricane. The whole town was destroyed. There were trees knocked down everywhere. We took a curve and then saw a thick forest in front of us.

"Go back," I said.

"Why?" asked Alice as she stopped the truck.

"We won't find the hurricane over here. If there are no trees knocked down, it *means the hurricane didn't go through here," I said.*

We turned back to where we came from and continued until we found trees knocked down again. We took a street that led us to a bridge. There were no trees beyond the bridge.

"Now, where do we go?" asked Steve.

"I checked the map. This street goes through a neighborhood surrounded by trees. If there are trees knocked down, we will know that the hurricane went this way," I said.

We continued driving until we saw several trees knocked down at the entrance to the neighborhood.

"It was here," said Alice.

"It's still here," I said, as I was looking right at a three-story house in the neighborhood.

We parked the truck close to the house. We got out and carefully walked towards the three-story house. The front yard of the house had been destroyed. As we approached the house, we noticed a shadow passing by a window inside the house. As we prepared our weapons, all the windows of the house opened at the same time. A strong gust of wind quickly came out of the house and knocked us to the ground.

The wind formed into the hurricane. Steve shot the formula at the hurricane. The formula passed through the wind as if nothing was there.

The hurricane formed a hand with its wind. It raised its hand of wind above the house and sucked it up. The hurricane formed another hand of wind. It pointed it at another house and threw a gust of wind at the house so strong that it pushed the house underground.

I stood up and ran towards the hurricane.

"Dr. Pren, what are you doing!" yelled Alice.

I went into the hurricane. Right away, I was swept up by the wind as it moved in circles at an incredible speed. Soon, I noticed that I could move. I tried to swim *through the wind towards the center of the hurricane, but I wasn't able to get far.*

Meanwhile, Alice kept shooting the formula at the hurricane without any success. Then, the hurricane started to absorb everything around it.

I crashed into a bed. Right away, I saw a wall passing over me. I noticed that the farthest end of the wall was near the center of the hurricane. I grabbed onto the wall and climbed up on it. I started to crawl on the wall to the other end but the wind started to rotate so fast that it made me faint.

Later, I started to hear Alice's voice. When I opened my eyes, I saw Alice right in front of me. I immediately noticed that Steve and Windor were there too. Now all four of us were flying in the hurricane.

"How did you get here?" I asked.

"Doing the same thing you did," said Windor.

"First of all, why did you get into the hurricane?" asked Steve.

"The wind that forms the hurricane comes from a source. If we destroy the source, the hurricane will disappear. The source must be in the eye of the hurricane," I said.

Suddenly, I saw a black wall in front of me. I put my hands on the wall. Right away, my hands started to sink into the wall. The wall was sucking me in. I was sucked in completely and I came out on the other side of the wall. Now I was in a very calm place, without wind, and with glowing light. When I looked up, I noticed there was a giant eyeball. The eyeball was twice my size and was floating just above me.

"So, this is the eye of the hurricane," I said.

The eyeball spun around, looking at its surroundings. I put my hand in my pocket to get my weapon out, but it wasn't there anymore. Apparently, I'd lost it in the hurricane.

The eye turned its gaze towards me. Chills went up my spine. The pupil of the eyeball started to shine brighter and brighter. A lightning bolt shot out of the pupil. I quickly got out of the way of the lightning bolt.

The pupil turned towards where I was and shot another lightning bolt again. The lightning bolt passed right between my legs. I jumped towards the eyeball and grabbed onto the pupil.

I started to climb the eyeball holding on by my fingernails because the eyeball was slippery. The eyeball started to shake so aggressively that I flew out through the air. The eyeball started to shoot lightning bolts at me again, but it missed me every time. Then, the eyeball released a huge cloud of smoke.

I couldn't see anything. The eyeball shot a lightning bolt that grazed my shoulder and set my shirt on fire. Immediately, I ran out of the cloud of smoke, took off my shirt, and threw it at the eyeball. The pupil started shooting lightning bolts at my shirt until it disintegrated.

At that moment, I looked around. I had a feeling. I decided to let my body react instinctively.

I jumped on the eyeball and climbed up until I was on top of it. I took off my shoe and put it on the pupil of the eyeball. When the pupil shot another lightning bolt, the shoe caught on fire. So, the eyeball caught on fire. The eyeball started to shake so aggressively that the pupil separated slightly from the eyeball creating a little hole. I fell inside the eyeball through the little hole.

I landed on something sticky and slimy. I could see everything around me now that the eyeball was burning up. I'd done something stupid. Now, I was trapped inside the eyeball. Then, I saw the little hole in front of me in the distance. I ran towards the little hole as fast as possible, but just before I reached the little hole, the eye started to fall to the ground.

When the eyeball crashed to the ground, I bounced back to the other side of the eyeball. The eyeball lost control of the hurricane. The hurricane started to fade. Already on the ground, the eyeball started to spin. Meanwhile, I was bouncing from one side to the other inside the burning eyeball.

Then, I noticed that I was on fire. I tried to put out the fire with my hands. At that moment, the eyeball was sucked into the black wall, and then it was spit out on the other side towards the strong gust of wind that still remained from the hurricane. The damage to the eyeball caused by the fire and the wind gust destroyed the eyeball, setting me free. The wind gust put out the flames that were burning me.

The hurricane vanished completely, throwing everything it had absorbed in all directions. As I was thrown out, I crashed into a tree in the air and was knocked unconscious.

CHAPTER EIGHT

....

THE SECRET HIDEOUT

I opened my eyes slowly and saw a hole in a ceiling. I looked from left to right. I was lying on a bedroom floor inside a house.

I tried to stand up, but my burns hurt too much. I grabbed the door handle of a closet and stood up. Then, I heard someone knocking on the door of the bedroom. I opened the bedroom door.

A germ came into the bedroom and grabbed me. I opened the closet door, saw some scissors, and tried to grab them, but I couldn't. The germ pulled me very hard and threw me across the room. I hit the wall and fell to the ground. Then, I noticed that inside the closet, there were crafts.

I stood up and ran to the closet with all my might to grab the scissors, but the germ caught me again. I was able to grab a hot glue gun that was connected to an electrical outlet on the wall. The germ threw me to the ground, got on top of me, opened its mouth, and brought its mouth closer to my face. I pointed the hot glue gun at the germ and shot hot glue into the germ's mouth. The germ opened its mouth even more as if it was going to scream, but it did not make a sound. The germ closed its mouth and got off of me. I kept shooting hot glue at the germ until it ran away.

I threw the hot glue gun on the floor and walked down the stairs. I left the house. I walked down the street, stumbled and leaned on a pole to hold me up. I looked across the street and saw Elijah's truck parked in front of me.

I looked around to see if there were more germs nearby. Then, I noticed there was a sign attached to the pole with a photograph of me. The poster read, 'Wanted, Dead or Alive, preferably alive.'

The poster also included a list of the charges against me. Apparently, I had been sentenced to seven years in prison for lying to the authorities, and for blaming innocent people.

"Did I do that?" I asked myself, "I didn't think it was that bad."

I got in the truck and started driving when suddenly I heard an explosion below me. The truck went flying through the air.

The truck landed in the middle of a forest. I looked out the back window. I saw hundreds of germs running towards me. One of the germs was carrying dynamite.

"These germs never give up," I said and turned on the truck. The truck started, but it only advanced a few feet before shutting down completely.

"I'm not surprised," I said.

Then, I remembered there was a motorcycle in the back of the truck. I got on it and took off like a lightning bolt. I looked back and saw that I was getting away from the germs. The germs started to look smaller and smaller in the distance. As I turned my gaze forward, I realized that I was coming out of the forest.

Now, I was driving across a soccer field complex during a youth soccer tournament. I almost crashed into a family who was enjoying a picnic. By dodging the family, I entered a soccer field where they were playing a game. I was able to dodge all the kids, but when I left the field, I crashed into a sidewalk in the parking lot, was ejected from the motorcycle, and flew through the air.

I landed in front of some portable bathrooms. I immediately realized that one of those portable bathrooms was ours. I went into the portable bathroom and used my credential to open the secret passageway on the floor of the portable bathroom.

When the secret passageway opened, I fell and landed on a rocket. Immediately, the secret passageway closed. I got comfortable and then I pressed a button. The rocket was launched through an underground tunnel. Minutes later, the rocket stopped.

A secret passageway opened above me. When I left the secret passageway, I was in the backyard of one of our bases. I went into my office, but I couldn't find anybody. I went up to the second floor, no one was there either.

"Where is everybody?" I asked myself as I went down to the basement.

In the basement, I found three workers lying on the floor. I realized that there might be germs inside that base. I knew I needed to get a weapon right away. I looked everywhere and I finally saw a weapon that was lying at the other end of the basement. I grabbed the weapon and went up the stairs to the first floor.

I checked the radars to see if the germs were approaching, but none of the radars were working. I punched one of the radars, but nothing happened. I didn't know what to do. I was getting desperate. I was about to disconnect the radars when suddenly a radar started beeping. The radar was detecting a very intense force.

"That must be Gilbert," I said.

I pulled out a map and marked where the force was coming from. I went into the garage, got on a motorcycle, put away my weapon, and rode in the direction of Milworm.

Finally, I arrived at the place indicated on the map, which was a hotel in Milworm. It was nighttime when I arrived. I looked through the hotel's windows and realized that the hotel was the secret hiding place of the germs.

Some germs were studying the movements of humans on a television so that they could attack them more easily.

Suddenly, something touched my shoulder. I turned and saw Alice and the other workers.

"Where were you, Dr. Pren?" asked Alice.

"I'll tell you later. I suppose you have a plan," I said.

"Everybody will go into the germs' secret hideout at the same time. We will fight until somebody finds the king and destroys him," said Steve.

"Is that your plan?" I asked.

"Yes, I suppose," said Steve.

"If that's your best plan, we will do it," I said.

So, we surrounded the hotel. Alice was by my side.

"How did you all know to come here?" I asked.

"Our radars detected a very powerful force coming from this place," said Alice.

"It seems very strange that out of nowhere, Gilbert lets us know where he is," I said. "It's almost as if he wanted us to be here."

"Now!" yelled Steve and we all entered the hotel.

I broke through one of the windows and entered into a hallway carrying a small crossbow full of the formula. The hallway was full of germs. I kicked a germ that was in front of me and shot the formula at another germ that was next to me.

I started shooting at all the other germs. More germs started coming out from everywhere. I kept shooting, but finally, one of the germs grabbed me from behind, it picked me up in the air, and made me drop my weapon. My weapon fell to the floor and broke. All the formula that was in the weapon spilled on the floor making a hole in the floor.

I kicked the germ that was holding me up in the air, but it wouldn't let go of me. I scratched its eye and the germ let go of me. Then, I punched the germ and pushed it out of the hotel through a broken window.

I turned around and I kicked another germ behind me. The germ grabbed my leg and pulled me, causing me to lose my balance. I fell backward to the floor. The germ jumped on me and opened its mouth.

Tentacles came out of its mouth and wrapped around my head. The tentacles pulled my head towards the germ's mouth. The germ was about to sink one of his teeth into my head. I covered my head with my right hand as fast as I could. The tooth sunk into my hand.

Immediately, the germ started to absorb my health through my hand. My hand was turning pale, and all my fingernails started falling off. My hand started to get so thin that I could see my bones. Black spots started to appear on my hand.

I didn't want to imagine how that would feel all over my body. I wasn't going to let that germ keep absorbing my health. With my left hand, I yanked out one of its teeth and stabbed it in its back.

"How does that feel, huh?" I yelled at the germ as I yanked out another tooth. I stabbed its tooth in one of its tentacles. The germ let go of me and threw me towards another germ.

The other germ caught me. I tried to get away, but I couldn't move my right hand. My right hand wasn't reacting at all. Desperately, I pushed the germ into the hole in the floor.

The germ and I fell into the hole. One of the germ's tentacles came out of its mouth and pulled my hair. I punched the germ in its belly to let go of me, but it didn't. Finally, the germ and I crashed into the basement floor. The germ turned into ashes. Behind the ashes was Windor.

"Aren't you going to thank me?" asked Windor.

"Watch out!" I yelled, but it was too late.

A germ jumped on top of Windor and knocked him to the ground. Windor dropped his weapon. I grabbed Windor's weapon. I was about to shoot the germ that was on top of him when suddenly, another germ grabbed my arm and threw me against a wall. I went through the wall and fell to the ground. I got up quickly and shot the germ that threw me to the wall.

I was in a room that didn't seem to have any form of access, except through the hole that I had just made in one of the walls. I looked around the room and noticed the presence of a germ at the other end of the room. The germ was brown. The germ was bigger, stronger, more aggressive and more dangerous than the other germs.

"I am Gilbert," said the germ.

CHAPTER NINE

....

THE DEFEAT

"You look different than the pet I created," I said.

"I have evolved," said Gilbert.

I raised up my crossbow and pointed it directly at Gilbert.

"Be careful, Dr. Pren. Tell me, what are you going to do after you destroy me?" asked Gilbert. "If you destroy me, you won't have a job any longer, and you will become poor. None of this would have happened if you had just listened to me from the beginning."

"A year ago, Patty and I were just joking when we said that we were going to create an army to destroy you, but you apparently don't understand jokes," said Gilbert, "and you tried to destroy us without compassion."

"How was I supposed to know that you were joking if you were both acting like you were serious about it?" I asked.

"It's just that you're not patient, and you don't listen," said Gilbert. "Because of you, we had to come up with a plan to defend ourselves from you."

"Does that mean that everything you both did was to get to this moment?" I asked.

"Exactly," said Gilbert, "remember what Patty said to you, 'One day, there will be a whole army fighting against you.'"

"So?" I asked.

"Don't you understand? Everything that's happened and everything that's going to happen is part of a plan. It is a plan involving an entire army," said Gilbert.

"So, you planned all this?" I asked.

"Not everything. I had someone's help," said Gilbert.

"Who's that someone?" I asked.

"Before I tell you who it is, I'll tell you that this person was the one who brought me to this planet. Maybe you're a little bit confused," said Gilbert.

"I'm very confused. I thought I was the one who gave you life," I said.

"It's humanly impossible to bring something like me to life. Someone went to your apartment one day when you were out with the boys painting graffiti on the city walls. That person replaced what you were creating with Patty and me. We germs have never been exposed to such a polluted environment like the one here on Earth, and that caused us to develop a disease. To get rid of the disease, we transferred it to humans while absorbing their health and that restored our bodies from the damage caused by the disease. But when we seemed to be completely cured, we became sick again. So, we started absorbing the health of humans when we were healed. Soon, we realized that the more health we absorbed from humans, the more powerful we became. You thought you'd given us life, when in reality it was someone else who brought us to you from a very distant place," said Gilbert.

"Where is that place?" I asked.

"That's where the person who put me in your apartment comes from. That person brought many more like me," said Gilbert.

"Exactly where do you come from?" I asked.

"I told you. We come from the same place the person who put us in your apartment comes from," said Gilbert.

"And who is that person?" I asked.

"I don't have to tell you," said Gilbert.

"Tell me who it is!" I shouted.

"You see how you're not patient. No doubt, if you keep going like this, you're going to make my plan much easier," said Gilbert.

"Tell me!" I shouted.

"Since you're not patient, I won't tell you," said Gilbert.

I was about to shoot him when he spoke again.

"Stop. I'm going to give you two options," said Gilbert.

"I don't want to hear your options," I said.

"You have to make a decision. If you decide to destroy me, that might help me to continue with my plan. If you decide not to destroy me, that too might help me to continue with my plan," said Gilbert.

"The only way for you to know if your plan will continue is if you are alive. Until never, stinky monster," I said and I started shooting at him.

"You're dumber than I thought," said Gilbert laughing as he turned into ashes.

Right after I destroyed Gilbert, I reflected on what he had just said. When I shot him, he acted as if that was exactly what he wanted.

Then, I noticed that all the germs had disappeared from the hotel. The germs had disappeared from everywhere.

When I left the hotel, I was arrested. The police took my weapon and put me in a police car.

"Where are all my workers?" I asked.

"Everyone's in jail. They'll be locked up for five years," the police officer said.

"Because of me, Alice, Steve, Windor, and all my other workers are in jail," I said.

My right hand was still injured. I was sitting in my jail cell, all alone, just like the vision I had had when I was a kid.

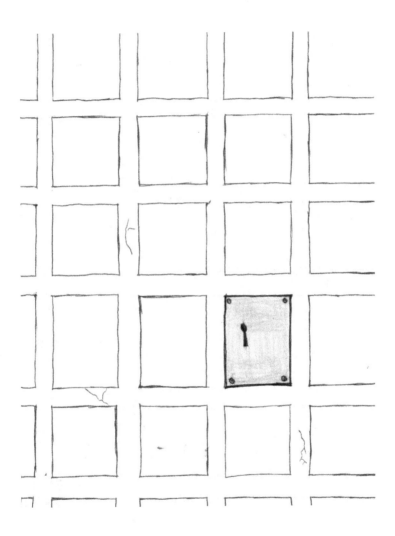

CHAPTER TEN

....

THE ENCOUNTER

"**W**ell, that's all for today," said Dr. Pren.

"Tell me a little bit more, please," said George.

"I'm tired. You'll have to come back tomorrow. I promise to tell you more surprising stories," said Dr. Pren.

"I don't like surprises," said George.

"My life is full of surprises. If you don't like surprises, I had better not tell you any more about my life," said Dr. Pren.

"All right, I'll wait until tomorrow," said George, "But it seems you still haven't told me much yet."

"Everything in time. See you tomorrow," said Dr. Pren.

"All right," said George.

The front door of the cabin opened on its own.

George left the cabin, and the door closed behind him.

George walked home. The humid air of the night wet his face. The silence and the darkness of the night covered his surroundings. George was so distracted thinking about what Dr. Pren had just told him that he didn't realize someone was coming towards him.

George bumped into the person. The person fell to the ground. It took a few seconds for George to realize what had happened. George helped the person stand up.

"I'm sorry, please forgive me. It's just that I'm having a crazy week and . . ." began to say George when the person interrupted him.

"Don't worry," said the person.

The person's voice was of a man, but his face wasn't visible in the darkness. George kept on walking as if nothing had happened. As George disappeared in the distance, the person turned and fixed his gaze on Dr. Pren's cabin with his snake eye.

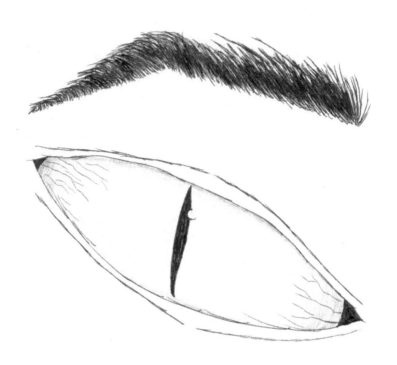

TO BE CONTINUED . . .

**Read all the books written by
Máximo César Castellanos**

Peter: A Chapter Book

~

Big Foot Hunting (Book 1)

Skeleton Wars (Book 2)

The Red Goblin (Book 3)

The Ghosts in My Attic (Book 4)

The Haunted Swamp (Book 5)

~

Dr. Pren and the Days of his Childhood
(Book 1)

Dr. Pren and the Attack of the Germs
(Book 2)

ABOUT THE AUTHOR

Máximo was born in Delaware.

At the age of 3, Máximo began creating stories through drawings. At the age of 4, Máximo discovered comics. Once Máximo learned to read and write, he began to write chapter books. Máximo is now 12 years old. He likes to read stories, invent stories, and write stories. He also enjoys creating illustrations, comics, and short films.

CPSIA information can be obtained
at www.ICGtesting.com
Printed in the USA
JSHW021629161022
31280JS00005B/54